DOWNERS GROVE PUBLIC LIBRARY

3 1191 00816 2703

W9-BPM-825

JUNIOR ROOM
DOWNERS GROVE PUBLIC LIBRARY

WITHDRAWN
DOWNERS GROVE PUBLIC LIBRARY

J/COMIC X-MEN
Grayson, Devin K.
Hearing things

Downers Grove Public Library
1050 Curtiss St.
Downers Grove, IL 60515

3/10-11
1V06-3

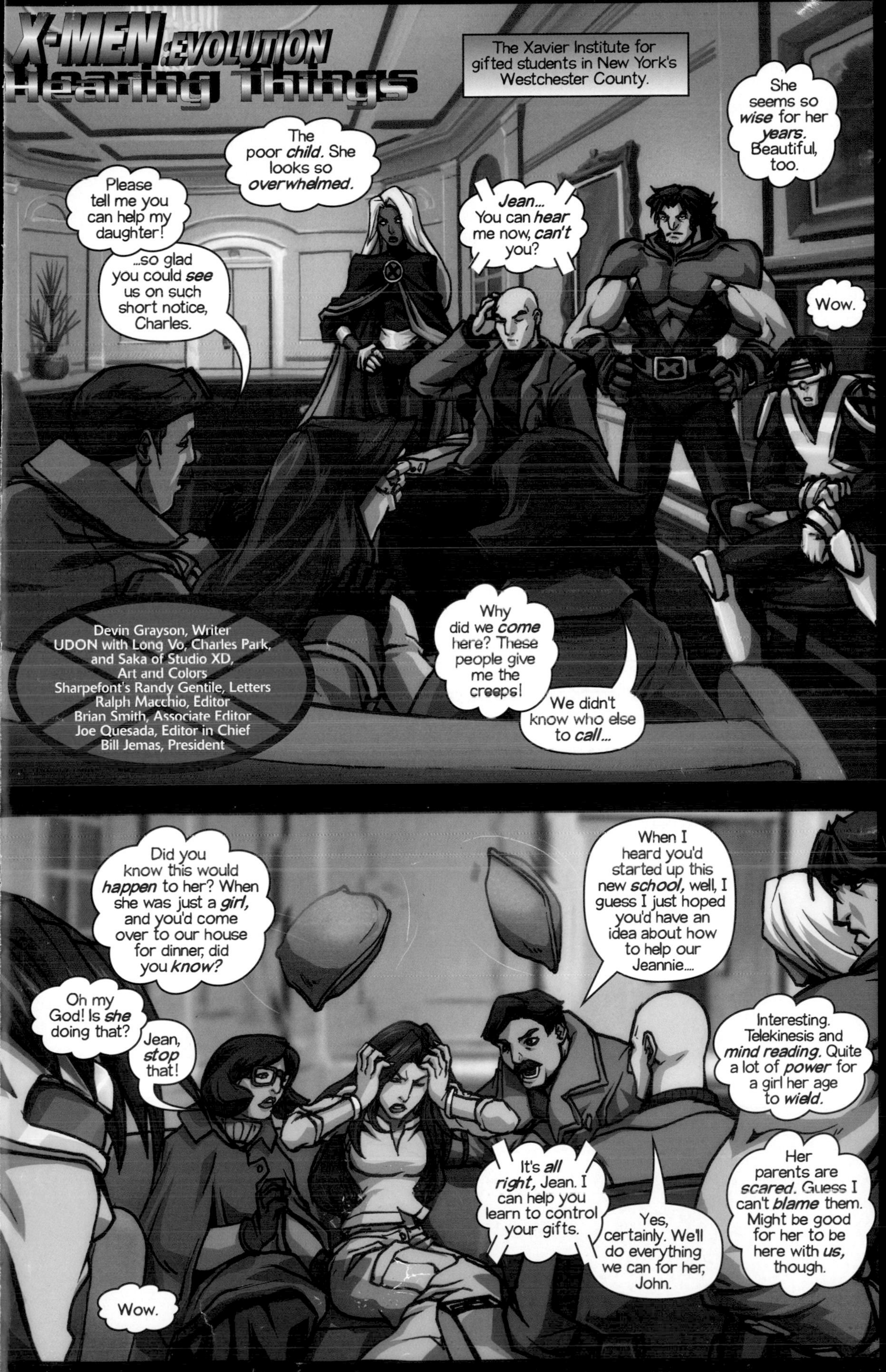
X-MEN: EVOLUTION
Hearing Things
The Xavier Institute for gifted students in New York's Westchester County.
Please tell me you can help my daughter!
...so glad you could see us on such short notice, Charles.
The poor child. She looks so overwhelmed.
Jean... You can hear me now, can't you?
She seems so wise for her years. Beautiful, too.
Wow.
Why did we come here? These people give me the creeps!
We didn't know who else to call...
Devin Grayson, Writer
UDON with Long Vo, Charles Park, and Saka of Studio XD, Art and Colors
Sharpefont's Randy Gentile, Letters
Ralph Macchio, Editor
Brian Smith, Associate Editor
Joe Quesada, Editor in Chief
Bill Jemas, President
Did you know this would happen to her? When she was just a girl, and you'd come over to our house for dinner, did you know?
When I heard you'd started up this new school, well, I guess I just hoped you'd have an idea about how to help our Jeannie....
Oh my God! Is she doing that?
Jean, stop that!
Interesting. Telekinesis and mind reading. Quite a lot of power for a girl her age to wield.
It's all right, Jean. I can help you learn to control your gifts.
Yes, certainly. We'll do everything we can for her, John.
Her parents are scared. Guess I can't blame them. Might be good for her to be here with us, though.
Wow.

VISIT US AT
www.abdopub.com

Spotlight, a division of ABDO Publishing Company Inc., is the school and library distributor of the Marvel Entertainment books.

Library bound edition © 2006

MARVEL, and all related character names and the distinctive likenesses thereof are trademarks of Marvel Characters, Inc., and is/are used with permission. Copyright © 2005 Marvel Characters, Inc. All rights reserved. www.marvel.com

MARVEL, X-Man: TM & © 2005 Marvel Characters, Inc. All rights reserved. www.marvel.com. This book is produced under license from Marvel Characters, Inc.

Library of Congress Cataloging-in-Publication Data

Hearing Things

ISBN 1-59961-053-1   (Reinforced Library Bound Edition)

All Spotlight books are reinforced library binding and manufactured in the United States of America

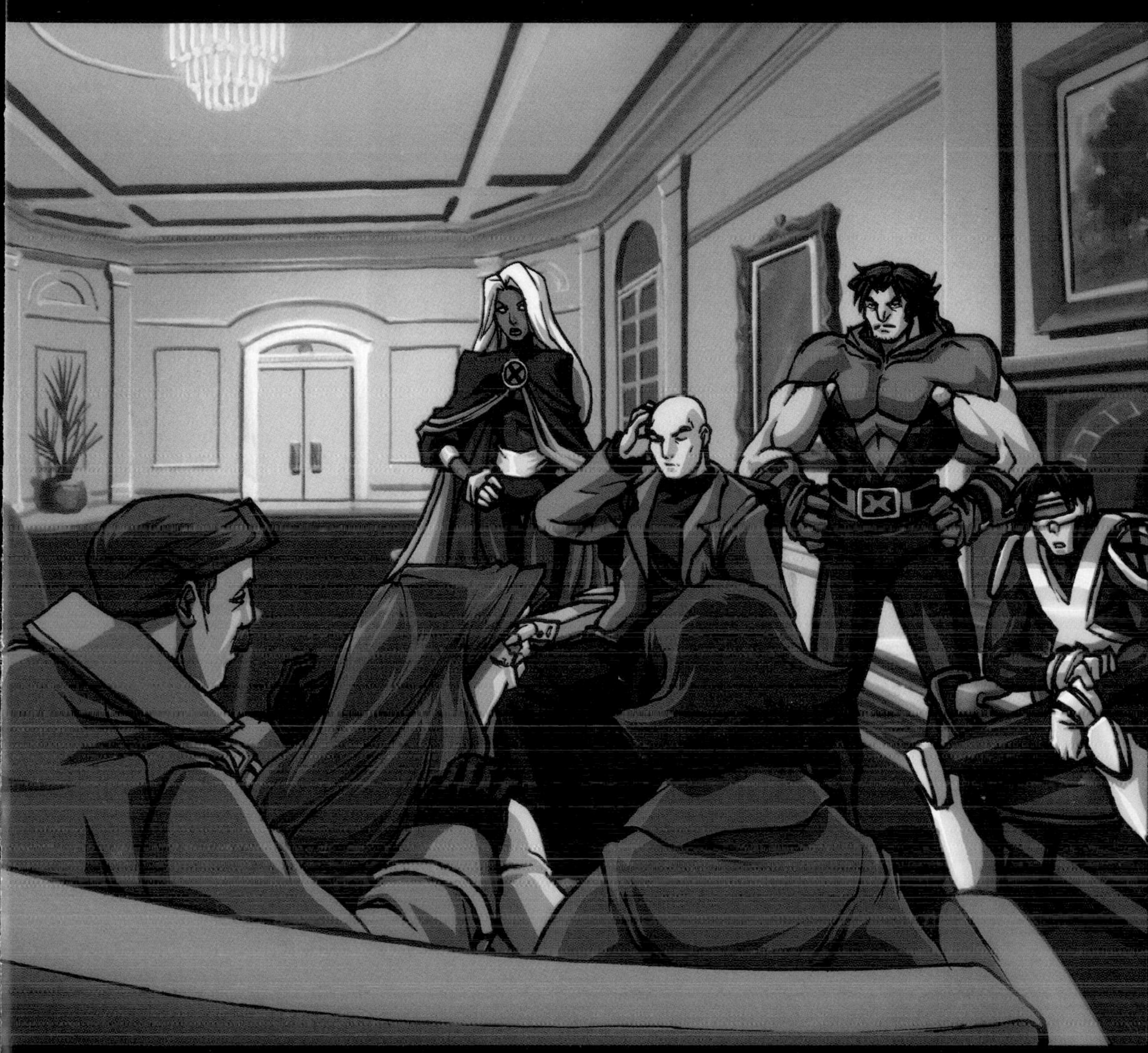
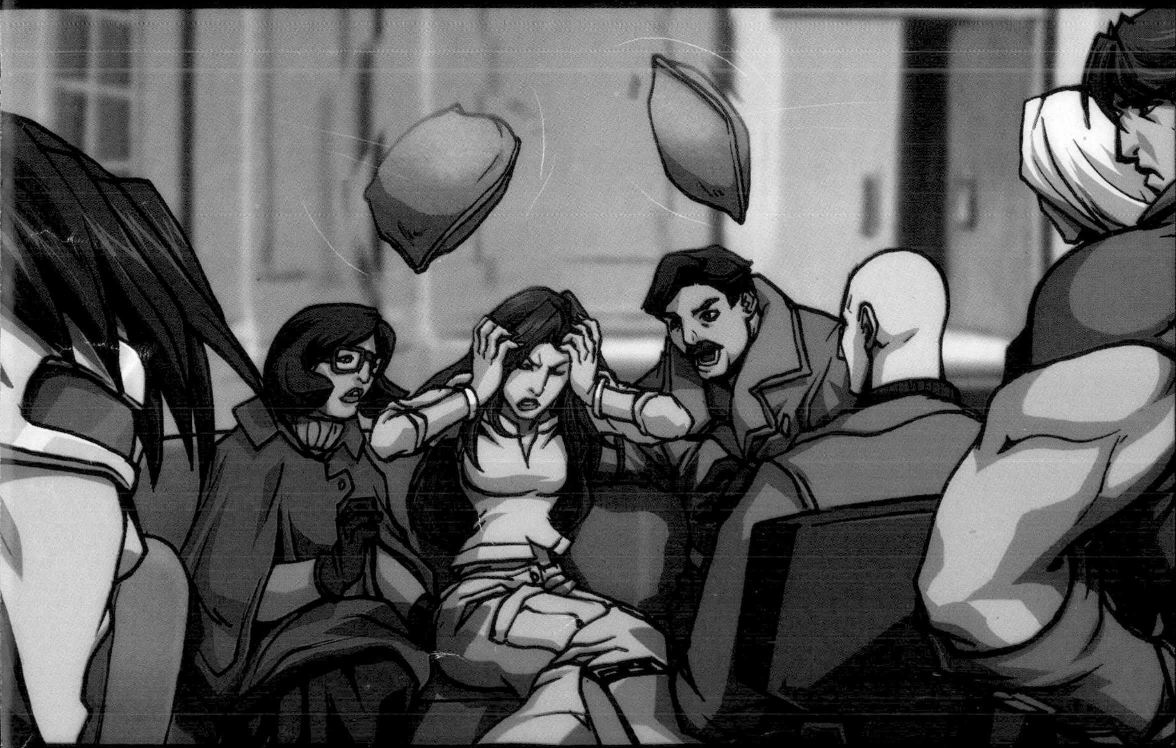

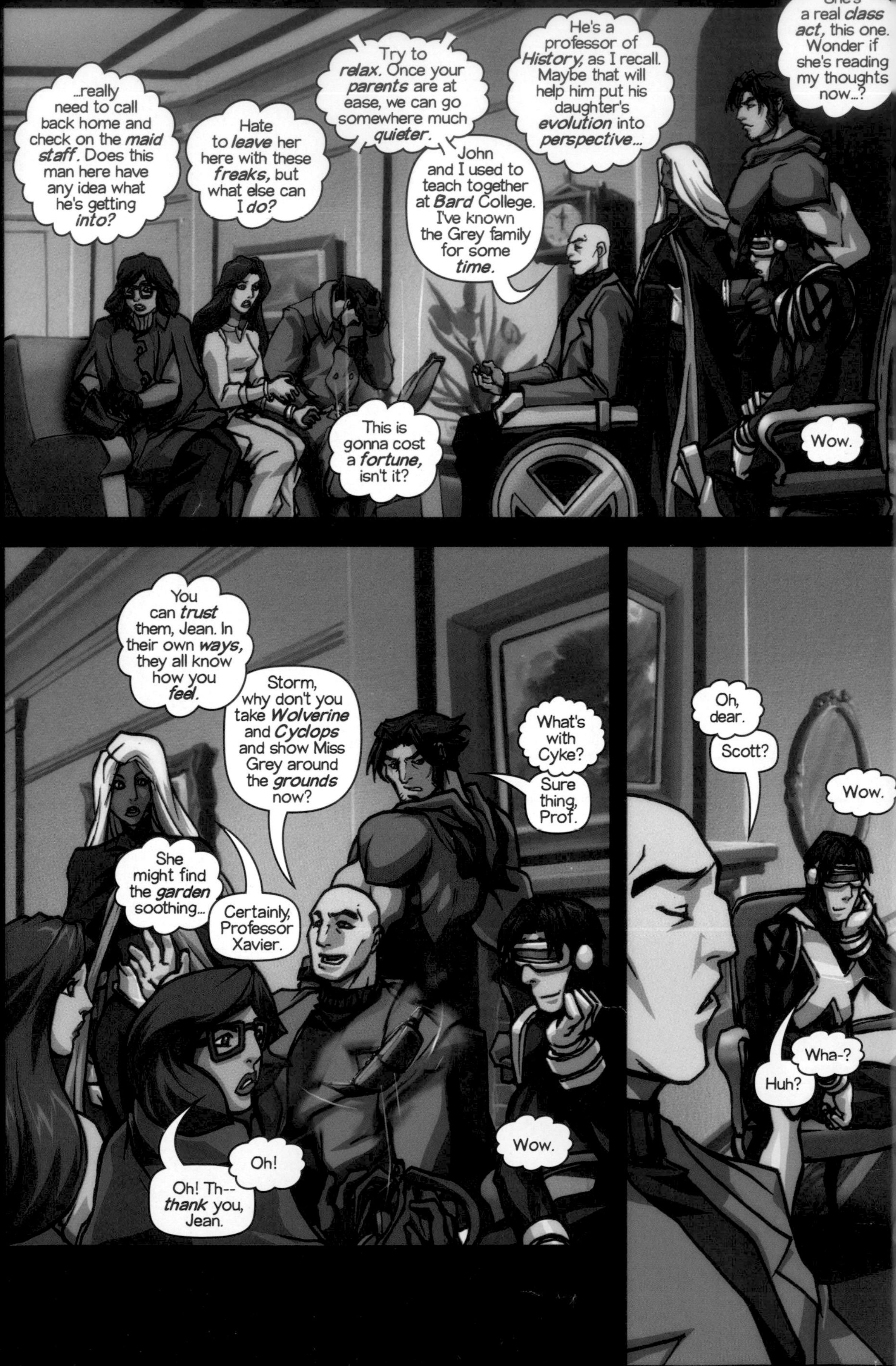

...really need to call back home and check on the maid staff. Does this man here have any idea what he's getting into?
Hate to leave her here with these freaks, but what else can I do?
Try to relax. Once your parents are at ease, we can go somewhere much quieter.
He's a professor of History, as I recall. Maybe that will help him put his daughter's evolution into perspective...
She's a real class act, this one. Wonder if she's reading my thoughts now...?
John and I used to teach together at Bard College. I've known the Grey family for some time.
This is gonna cost a fortune, isn't it?
Wow.
You can trust them, Jean. In their own ways, they all know how you feel.
Storm, why don't you take Wolverine and Cyclops and show Miss Grey around the grounds now?
What's with Cyke?
Sure thing, Prof.
She might find the garden soothing...
Certainly, Professor Xavier.
Oh!
Oh! Th-- thank you, Jean.
Wow.
Oh, dear.
Scott?
Wow.
Wha-?
Huh?

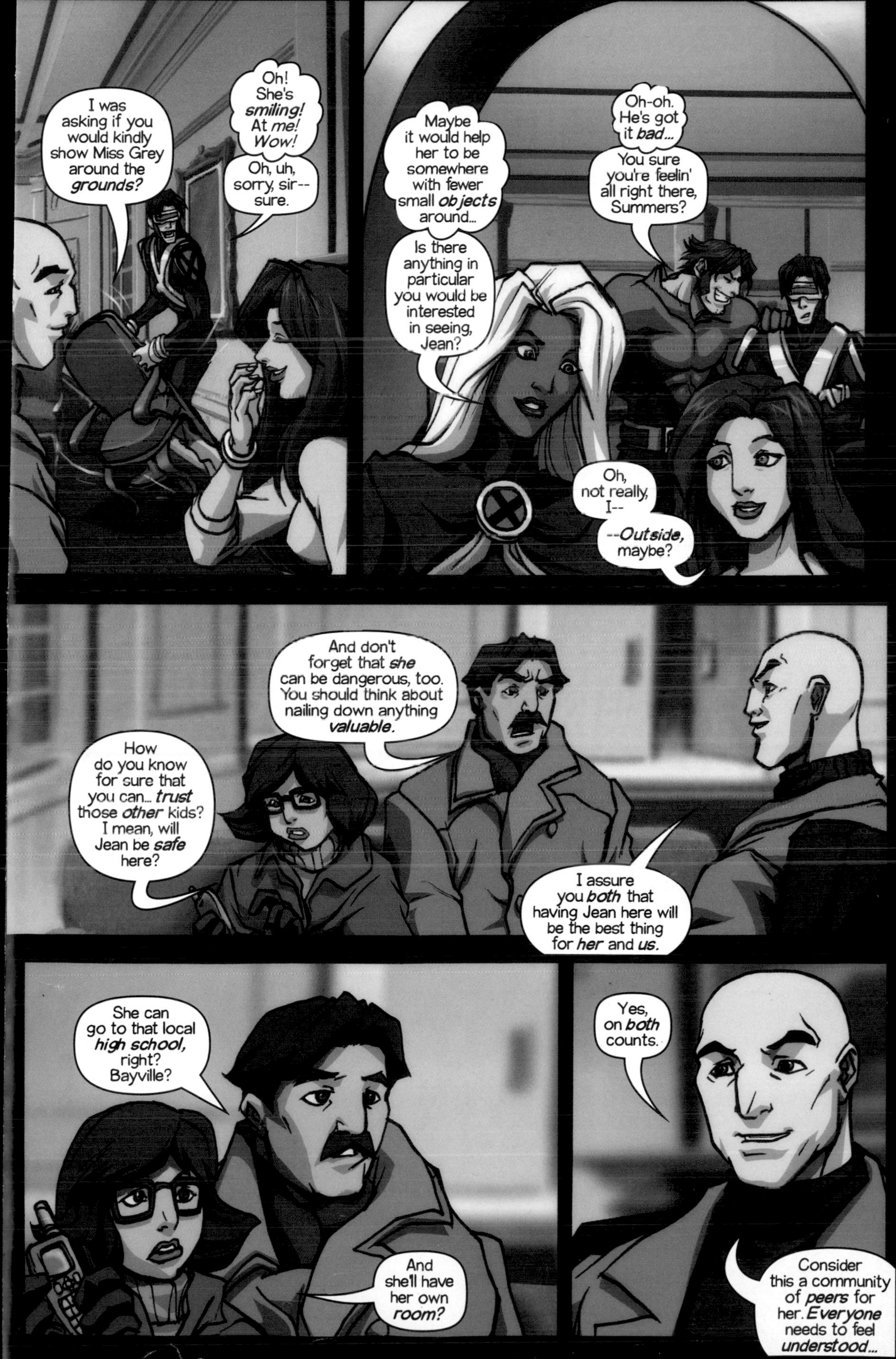
I was asking if you would kindly show Miss Grey around the *grounds?*
Oh! She's *smiling!* At *me!* *Wow!*
Oh, uh, sorry, sir-- sure.
Maybe it would help her to be somewhere with fewer small *objects* around...
Is there anything in particular you would be interested in seeing, Jean?
Oh-oh. He's got it *bad...*
You sure you're feelin' all right there, Summers?
Oh, not really, I--
--*Outside,* maybe?
How do you know for sure that you can... *trust* those *other* kids? I mean, will Jean be *safe* here?
And don't forget that *she* can be dangerous, too. You should think about nailing down anything *valuable.*
I assure you *both* that having Jean here will be the best thing for *her* and *us.*
She can go to that local *high school,* right? Bayville?
And she'll have her own *room?*
Yes, on *both* counts.
Consider this a community of *peers* for her. *Everyone* needs to feel *understood...*

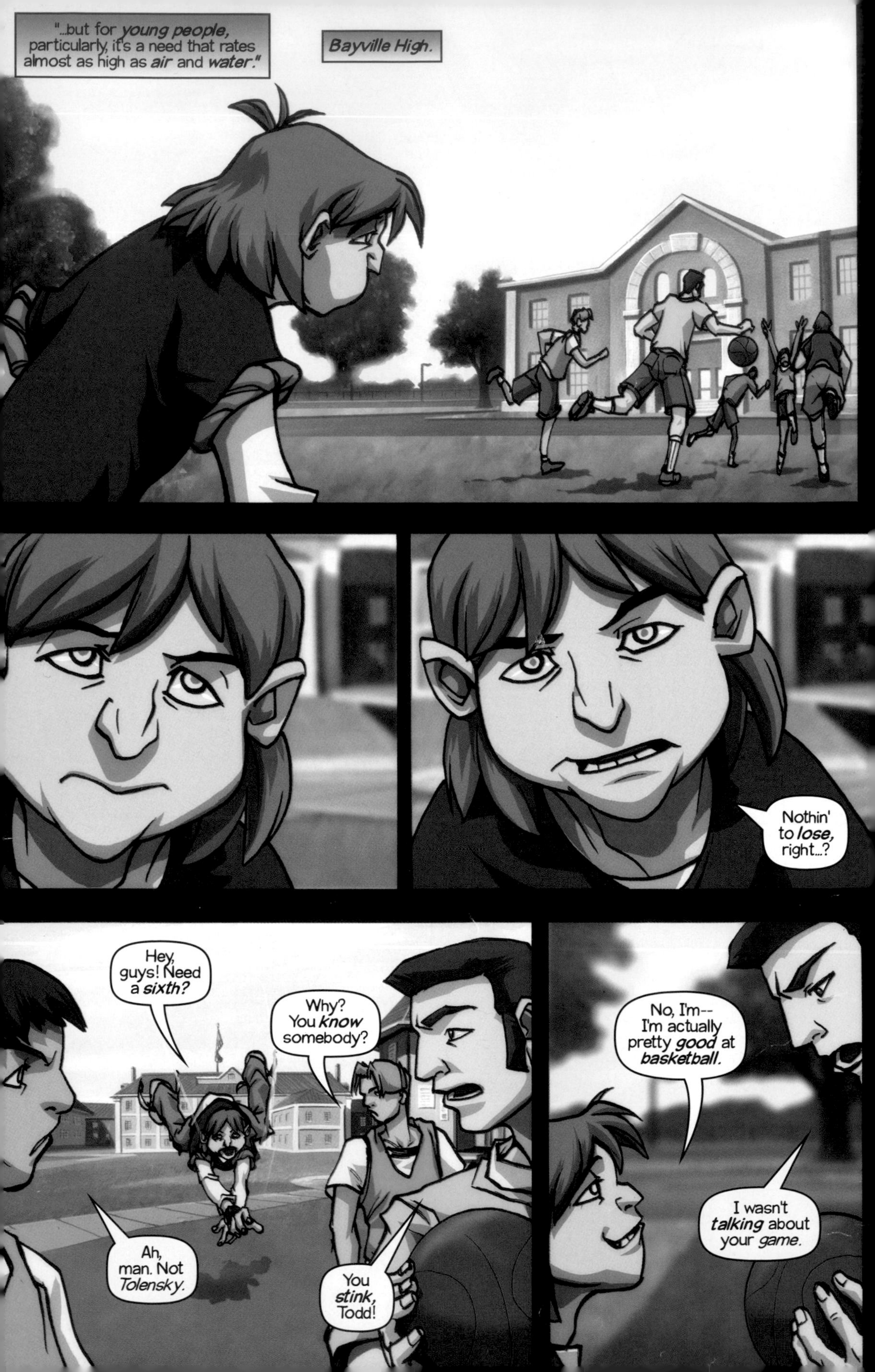

"...but for young people, particularly, it's a need that rates almost as high as air and water."
Bayville High.
Nothin' to lose, right...?
Hey, guys! Need a sixth?
Why? You know somebody?
Ah, man. Not Tolensky.
You stink, Todd!
No, I'm-- I'm actually pretty good at basketball.
I wasn't talking about your game.

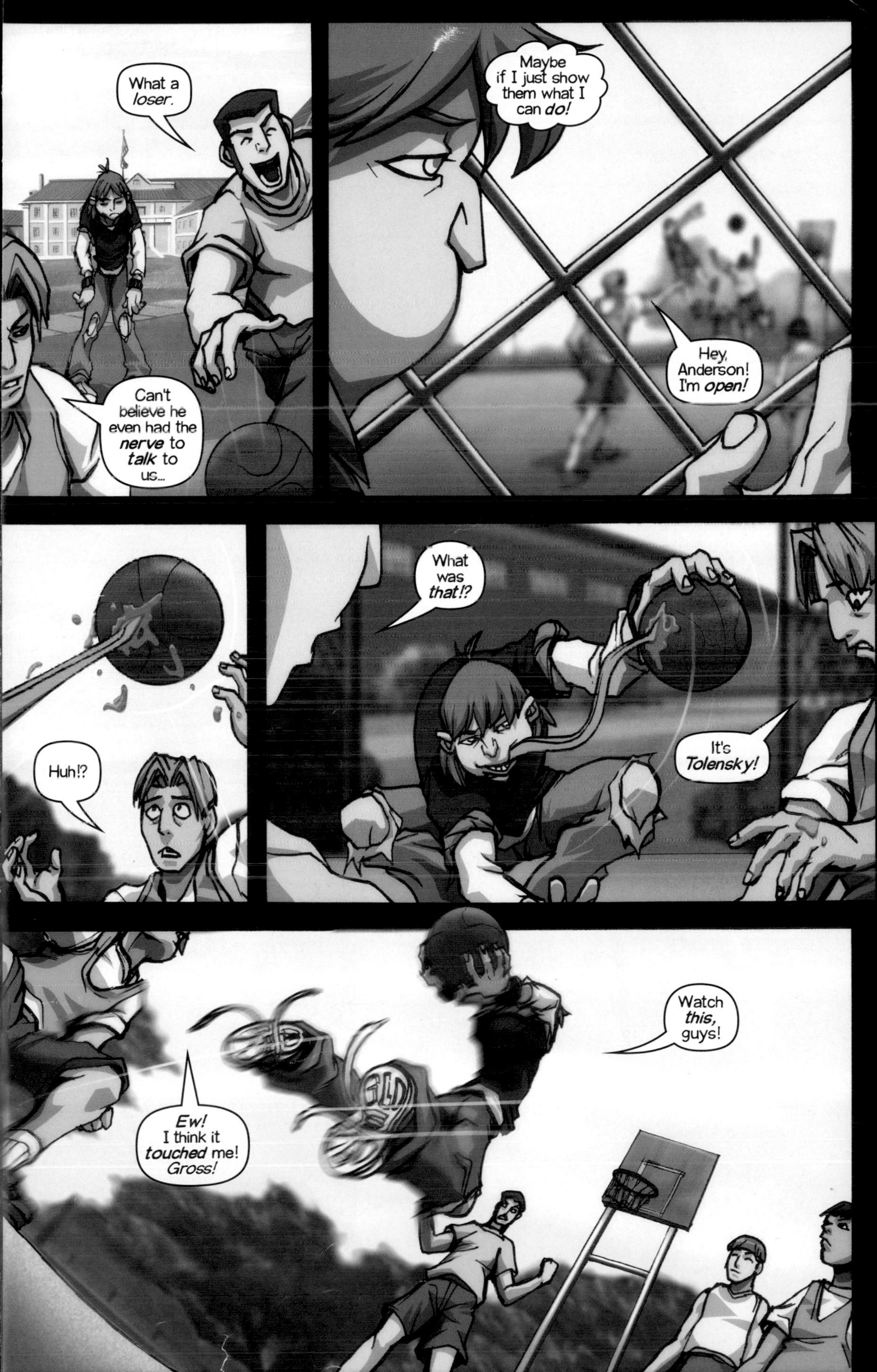
What a *loser.*
Can't believe he even had the *nerve* to *talk* to us...
Maybe if I just show them what I can *do!*
Hey, Anderson! I'm *open!*
Huh!?
What was *that!?*
It's *Tolensky!*
Watch *this,* guys!
Ew! I think it *touched* me! *Gross!*

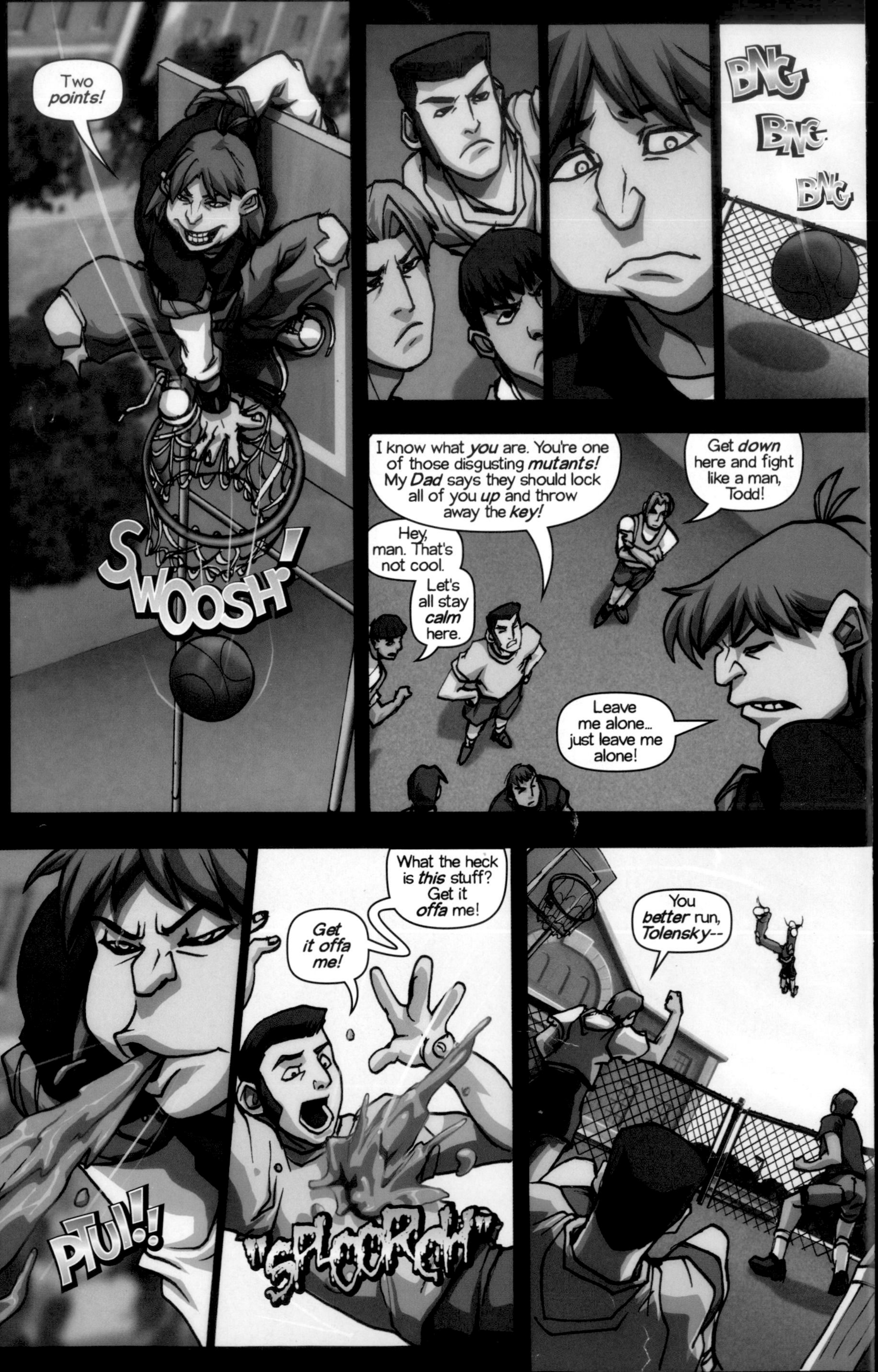

Two points!
SWOOSH!
BNG
BNG
BNG
I know what you are. You're one of those disgusting mutants! My Dad says they should lock all of you up and throw away the key!
Get down here and fight like a man, Todd!
Hey, man. That's not cool.
Let's all stay calm here.
Leave me alone... just leave me alone!
PTUI!!
What the heck is this stuff? Get it offa me!
Get it offa me!
SPLOORCH
You better run, Tolensky--

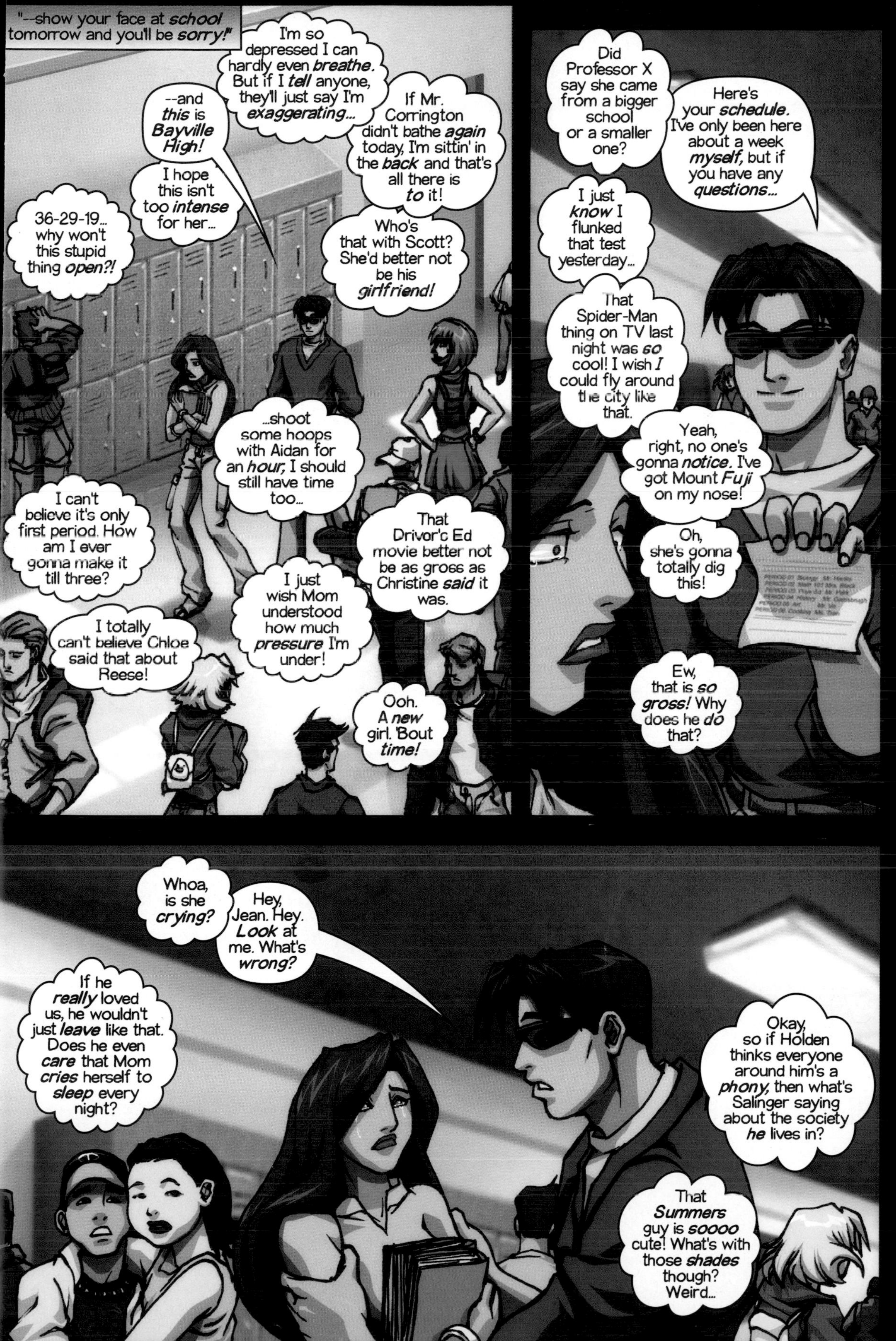
"--show your face at school tomorrow and you'll be sorry!"
I'm so depressed I can hardly even breathe. But if I tell anyone, they'll just say I'm exaggerating...
--and this is Bayville High!
I hope this isn't too intense for her...
If Mr. Corrington didn't bathe again today, I'm sittin' in the back and that's all there is to it!
36-29-19... why won't this stupid thing open?!
Who's that with Scott? She'd better not be his girlfriend!
...shoot some hoops with Aidan for an hour, I should still have time too...
I can't believe it's only first period. How am I ever gonna make it till three?
That Drivor's Ed movie better not be as gross as Christine said it was.
I just wish Mom understood how much pressure I'm under!
I totally can't believe Chloe said that about Reese!
Ooh. A new girl. 'Bout time!
Did Professor X say she came from a bigger school or a smaller one?
Here's your schedule. I've only been here about a week myself, but if you have any questions...
I just know I flunked that test yesterday...
That Spider-Man thing on TV last night was so cool! I wish I could fly around the city like that.
Yeah, right, no one's gonna notice. I've got Mount Fuji on my nose!
Oh, she's gonna totally dig this!
Ew, that is so gross! Why does he do that?
Whoa, is she crying?
Hey, Jean. Hey. Look at me. What's wrong?
If he really loved us, he wouldn't just leave like that. Does he even care that Mom cries herself to sleep every night?
Okay, so if Holden thinks everyone around him's a phony, then what's Salinger saying about the society he lives in?
That Summers guy is soooo cute! What's with those shades though? Weird...

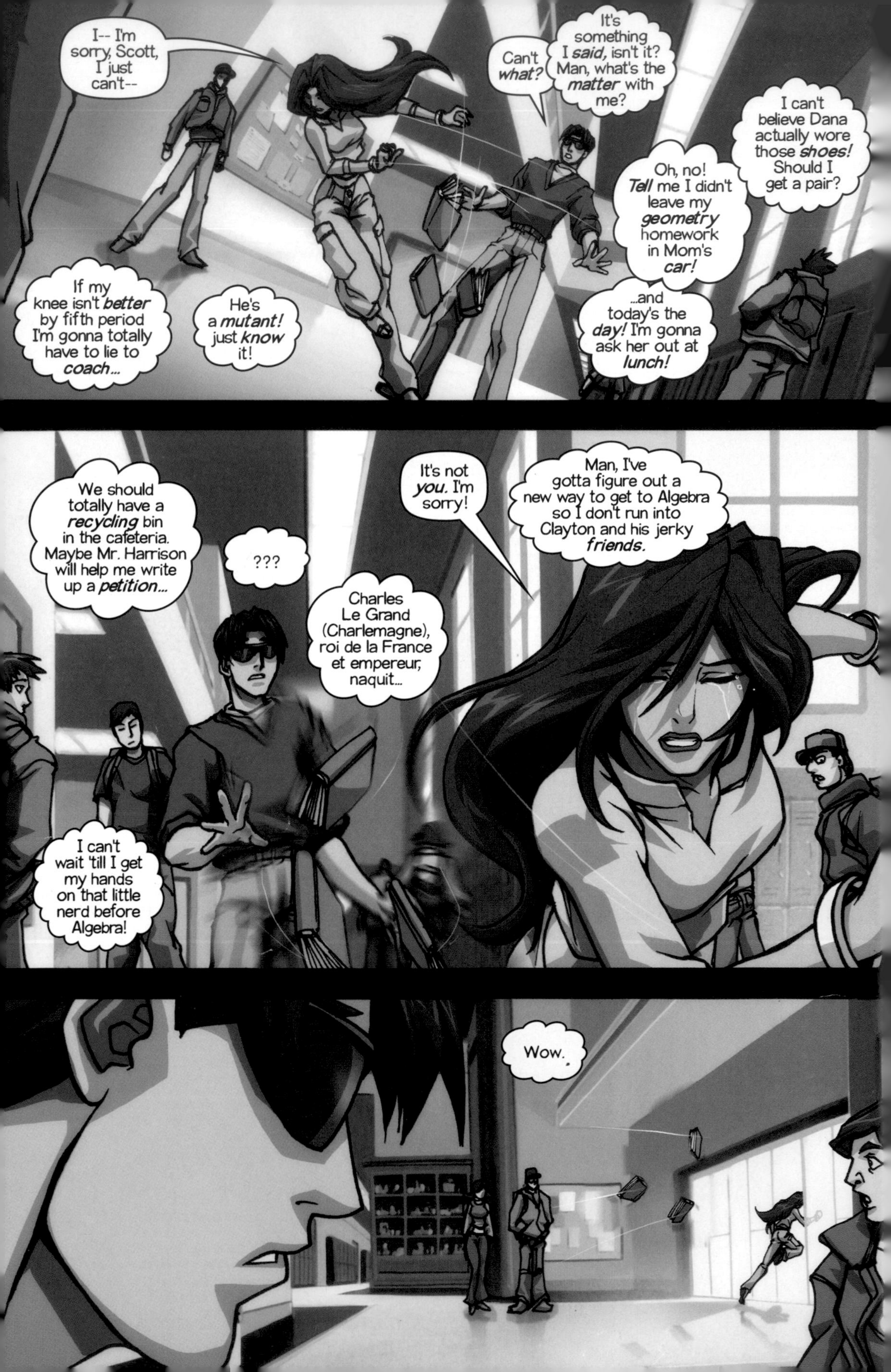
I-- I'm sorry, Scott, I just can't--
Can't *what?*
It's something I *said,* isn't it? Man, what's the *matter* with me?
I can't believe Dana actually wore those *shoes!* Should I get a pair?
Oh, no! *Tell* me I didn't leave my *geometry* homework in Mom's *car!*
If my knee isn't *better* by fifth period I'm gonna totally have to lie to *coach...*
He's a *mutant!* just *know* it!
...and today's the *day!* I'm gonna ask her out at *lunch!*
We should totally have a *recycling* bin in the cafeteria. Maybe Mr. Harrison will help me write up a *petition...*
???
It's not *you.* I'm sorry!
Man, I've gotta figure out a new way to get to Algebra so I don't run into Clayton and his jerky *friends.*
Charles Le Grand (Charlemagne), roi de la France et empereur, naquit...
I can't wait 'till I get my hands on that little nerd before Algebra!
Wow.

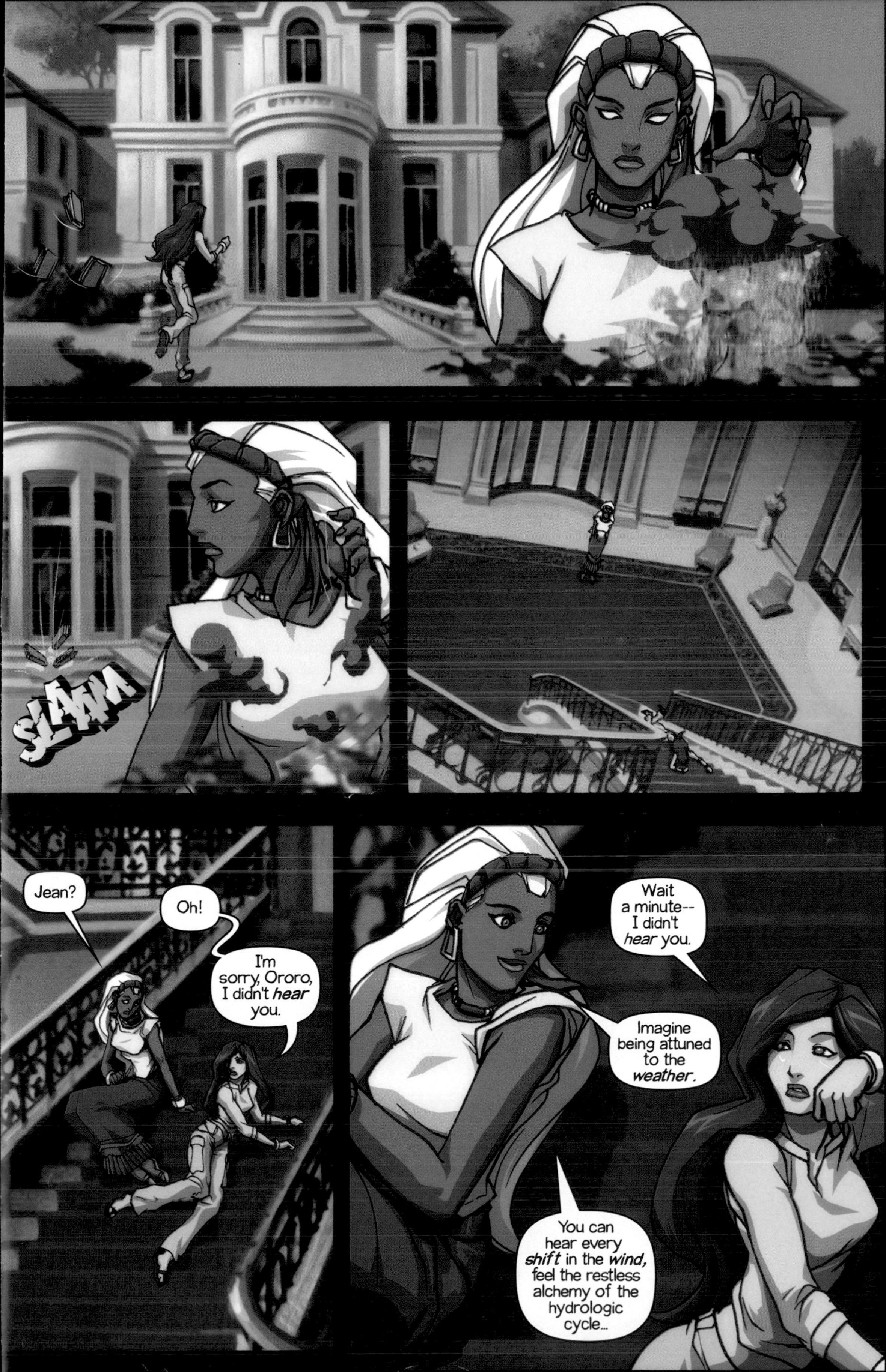
SLAMM
Jean?
Oh!
I'm sorry, Ororo, I didn't *hear* you.
Wait a minute-- I didn't *hear* you.
Imagine being attuned to the *weather.*
You can hear every *shift* in the *wind,* feel the restless alchemy of the hydrologic cycle...

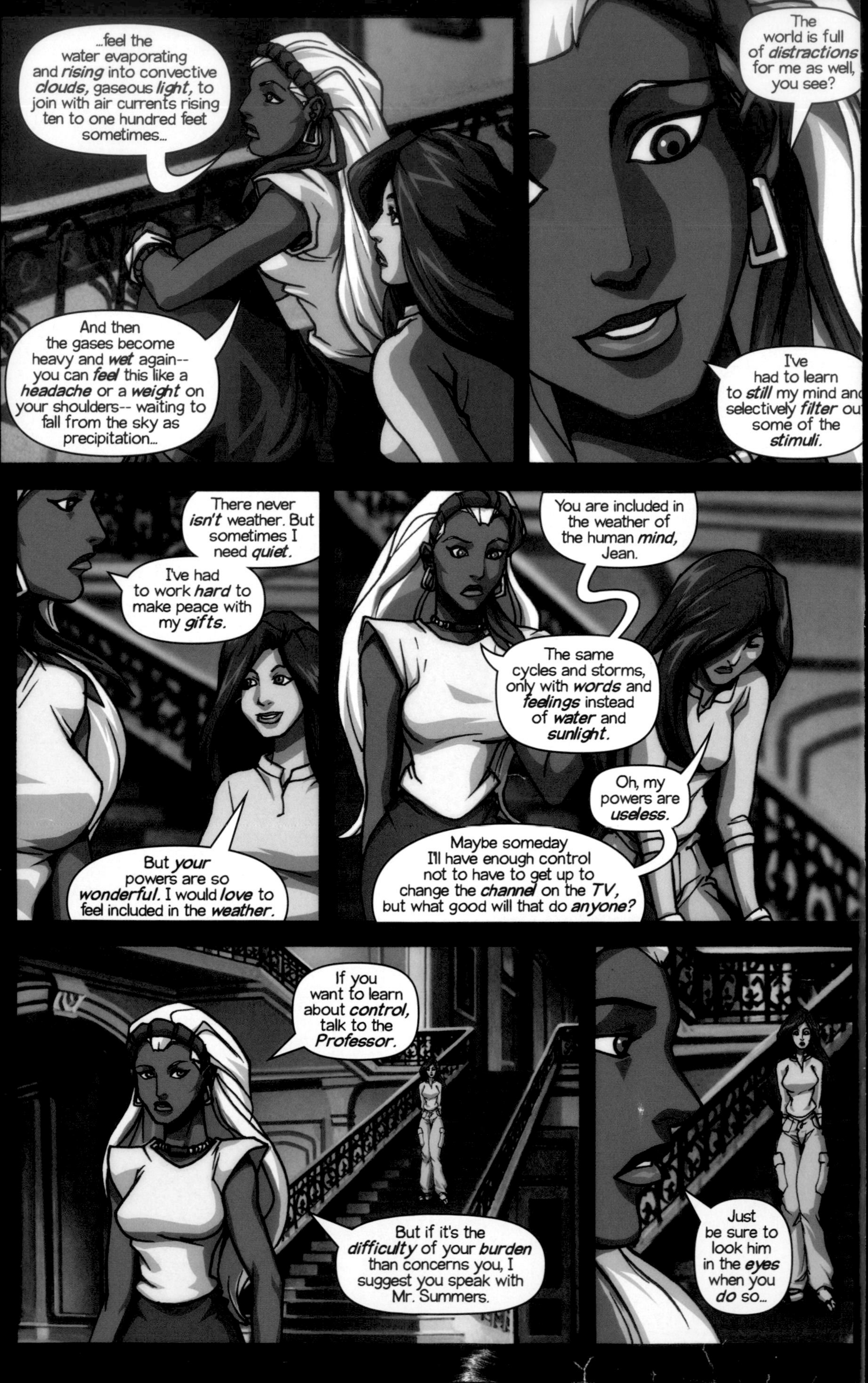
...feel the water evaporating and rising into convective clouds, gaseous light, to join with air currents rising ten to one hundred feet sometimes...
And then the gases become heavy and wet again-- you can feel this like a headache or a weight on your shoulders-- waiting to fall from the sky as precipitation...
The world is full of distractions for me as well, you see?
I've had to learn to still my mind and selectively filter out some of the stimuli.
There never isn't weather. But sometimes I need quiet.
I've had to work hard to make peace with my gifts.
But your powers are so wonderful. I would love to feel included in the weather.
You are included in the weather of the human mind, Jean.
The same cycles and storms, only with words and feelings instead of water and sunlight.
Oh, my powers are useless.
Maybe someday I'll have enough control not to have to get up to change the channel on the TV, but what good will that do anyone?
If you want to learn about control, talk to the Professor.
But if it's the difficulty of your burden than concerns you, I suggest you speak with Mr. Summers.
Just be sure to look him in the eyes when you do so...

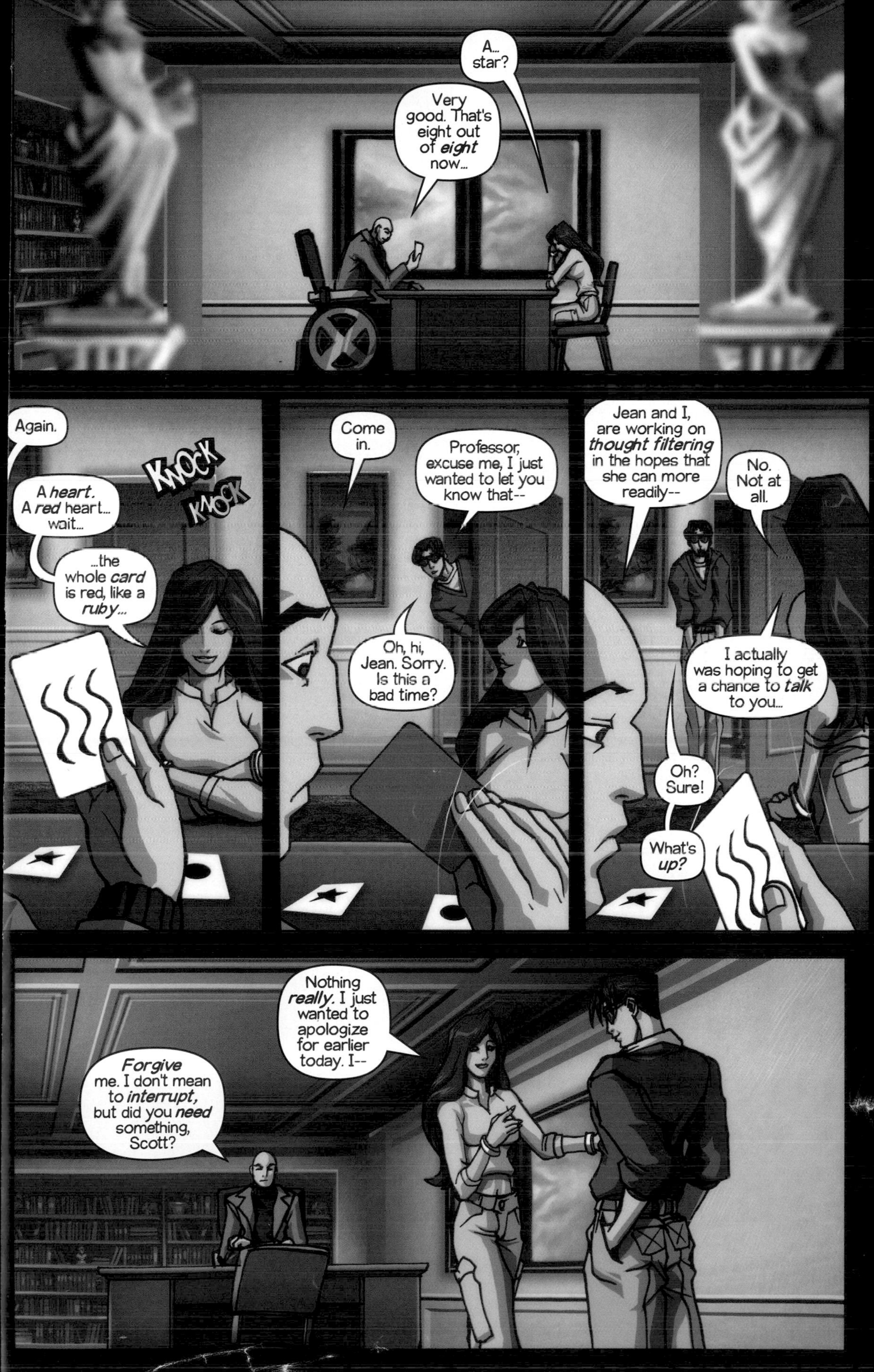
A... star?
Very good. That's eight out of *eight* now...
Again.
A *heart.* A *red* heart... wait...
...the whole *card* is red, like a *ruby*...
KNOCK KNOCK
Come in.
Professor, excuse me, I just wanted to let you know that--
Oh, hi, Jean. Sorry. Is this a bad time?
Jean and I, are working on *thought filtering* in the hopes that she can more readily--
No. Not at all.
I actually was hoping to get a chance to *talk* to you...
Oh? Sure!
What's *up?*
Nothing *really.* I just wanted to apologize for earlier today. I--
Forgive me. I don't mean to *interrupt,* but did you *need* something, Scott?

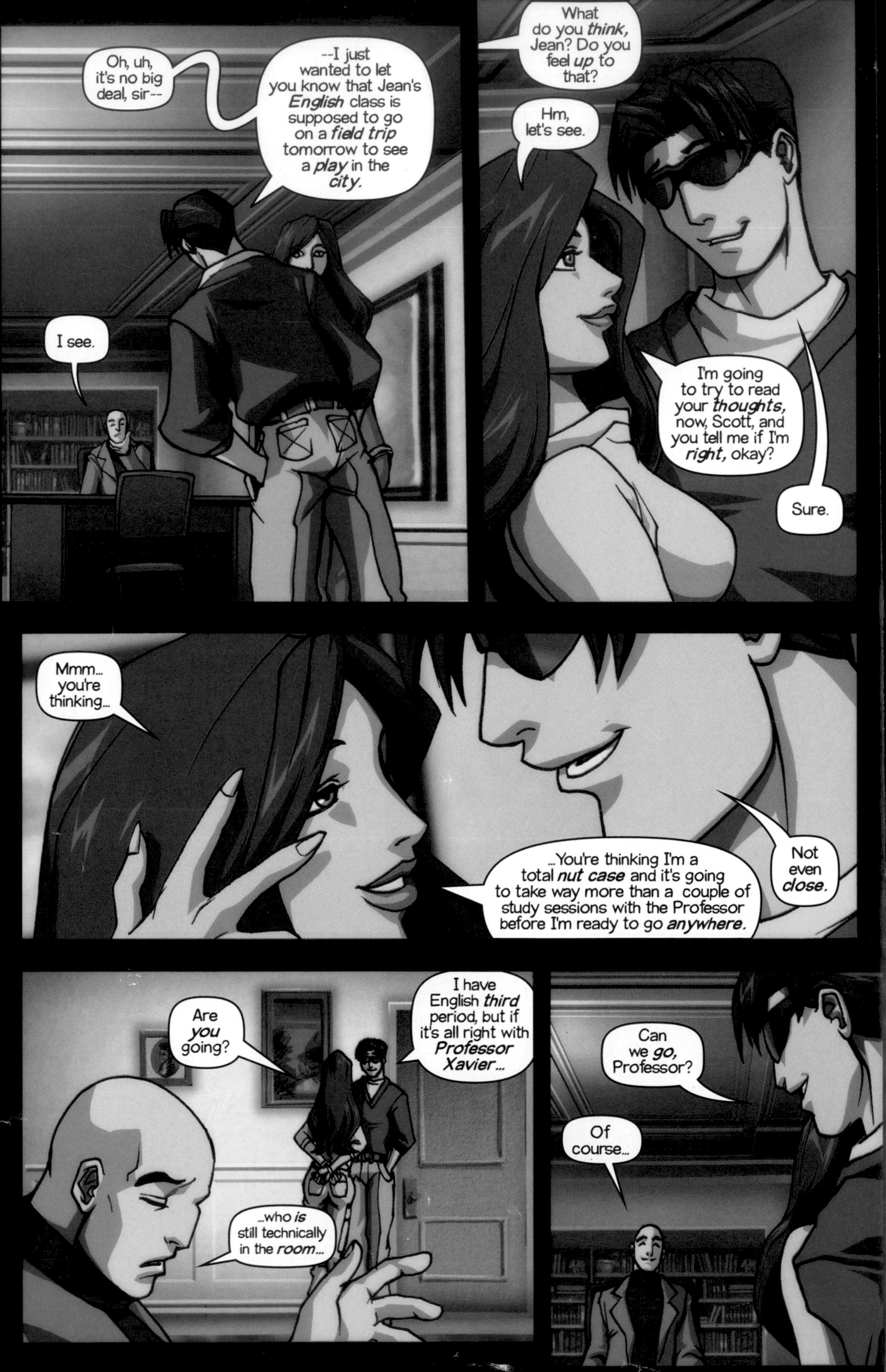
Oh, uh, it's no big deal, sir--
--I just wanted to let you know that Jean's *English* class is supposed to go on a *field trip* tomorrow to see a *play* in the *city.*
I see.
What do you *think,* Jean? Do you feel *up* to that?
Hm, let's see.
I'm going to try to read your *thoughts,* now, Scott, and you tell me if I'm *right,* okay?
Sure.
Mmm... you're thinking...
...You're thinking I'm a total *nut case* and it's going to take way more than a couple of study sessions with the Professor before I'm ready to go *anywhere.*
Not even *close.*
Are *you* going?
I have English *third* period, but if it's all right with *Professor Xavier...*
...who *is* still technically in the *room...*
Can we *go,* Professor?
Of course...

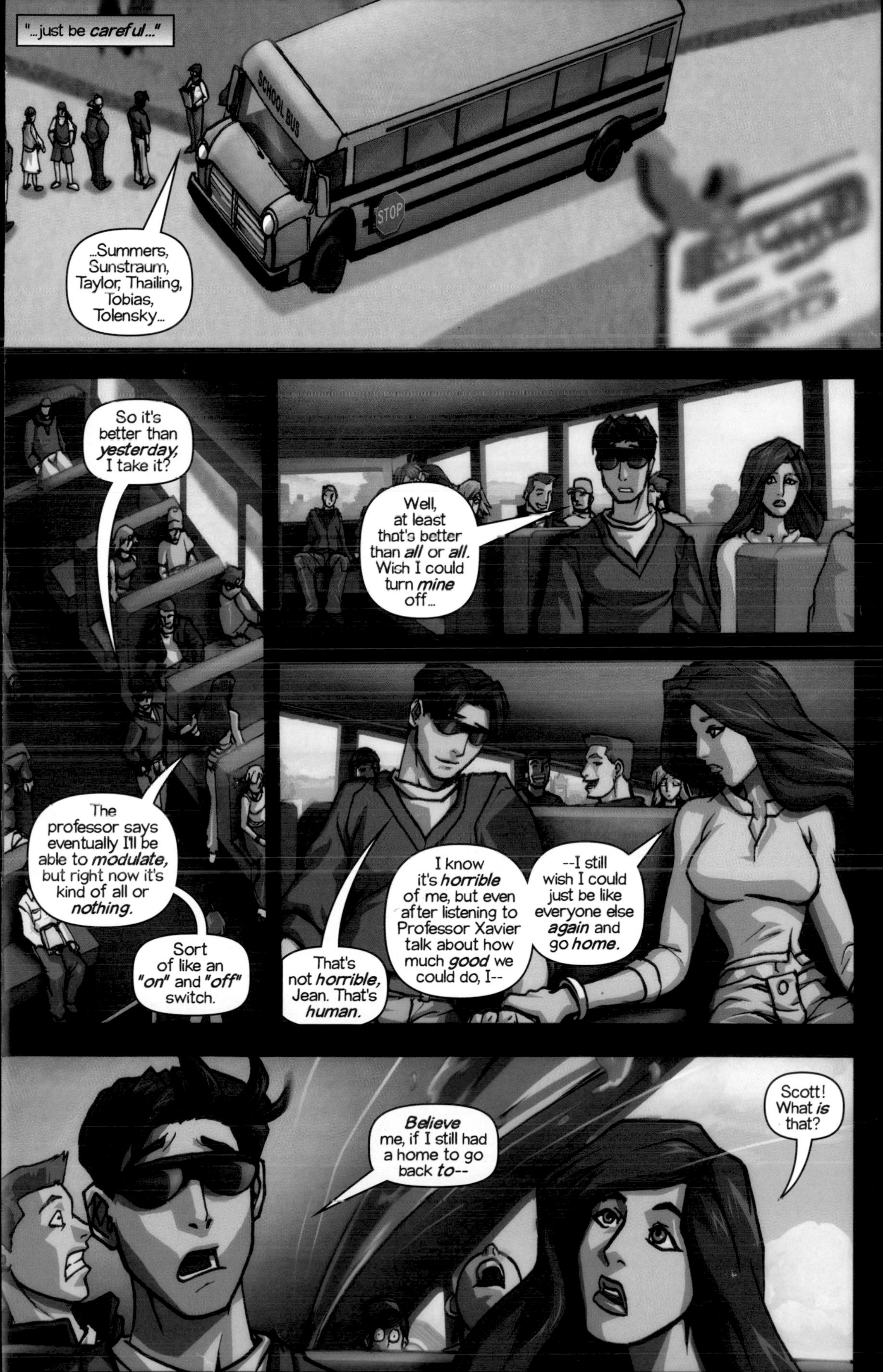
"...just be careful..."
...Summers, Sunstraum, Taylor, Thailing, Tobias, Tolensky...
SCHOOL BUS
STOP
So it's better than yesterday, I take it?
Well, at least that's better than all or all. Wish I could turn mine off...
The professor says eventually I'll be able to modulate, but right now it's kind of all or nothing.
Sort of like an "on" and "off" switch.
That's not horrible, Jean. That's human.
I know it's horrible of me, but even after listening to Professor Xavier talk about how much good we could do, I--
--I still wish I could just be like everyone else again and go home.
Believe me, if I still had a home to go back to--
Scott! What is that?

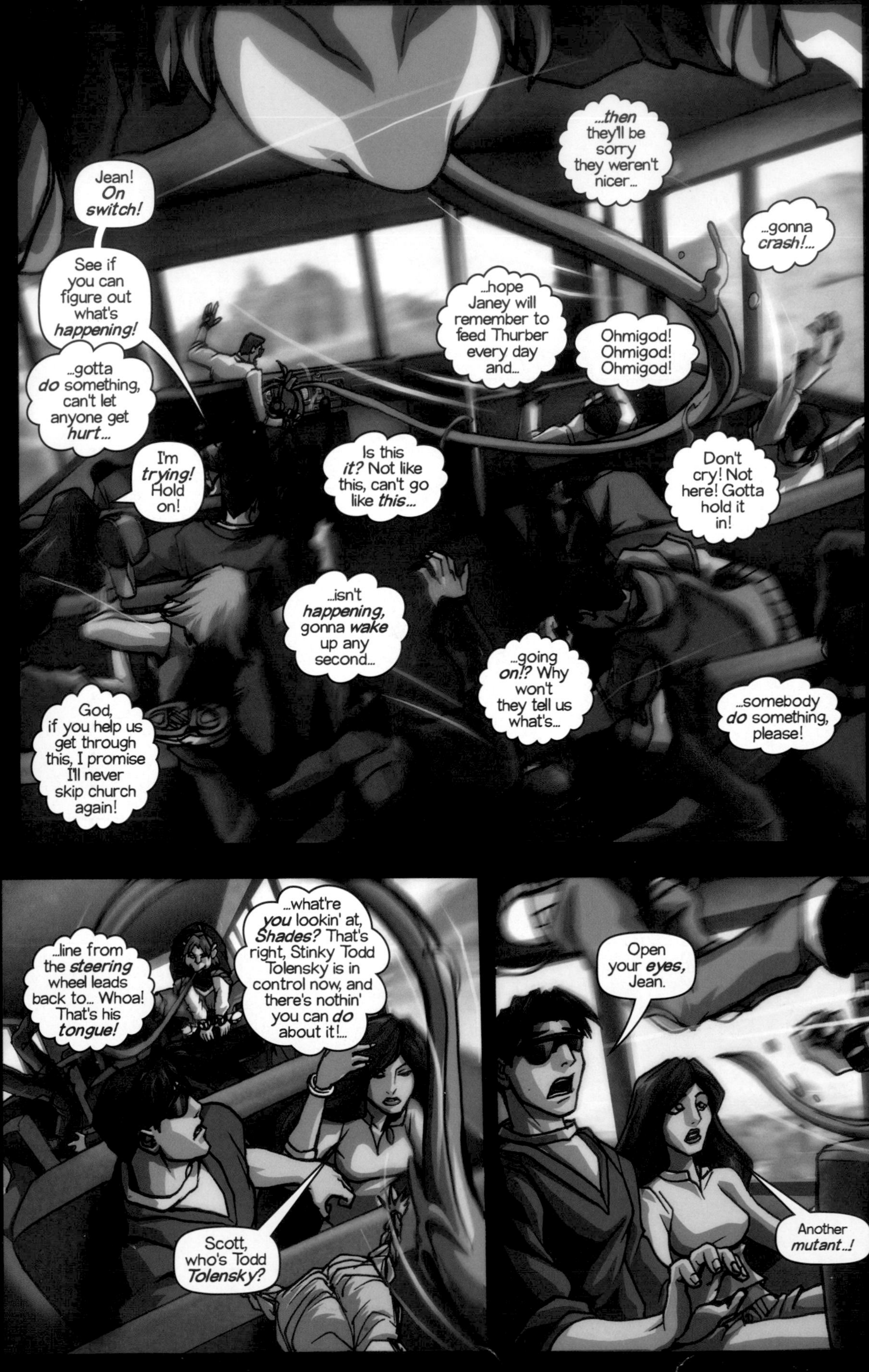

Jean! On switch!
...then they'll be sorry they weren't nicer...
...gonna crash!...
See if you can figure out what's happening!
...hope Janey will remember to feed Thurber every day and...
Ohmigod! Ohmigod! Ohmigod!
...gotta do something, can't let anyone get hurt...
I'm trying! Hold on!
Is this it? Not like this, can't go like this...
Don't cry! Not here! Gotta hold it in!
...isn't happening, gonna wake up any second...
...going on!? Why won't they tell us what's...
...somebody do something, please!
God, if you help us get through this, I promise I'll never skip church again!
...line from the steering wheel leads back to... Whoa! That's his tongue!
...what're you lookin' at, Shades? That's right, Stinky Todd Tolensky is in control now, and there's nothin' you can do about it!...
Scott, who's Todd Tolensky?
Open your eyes, Jean.
Another mutant..!

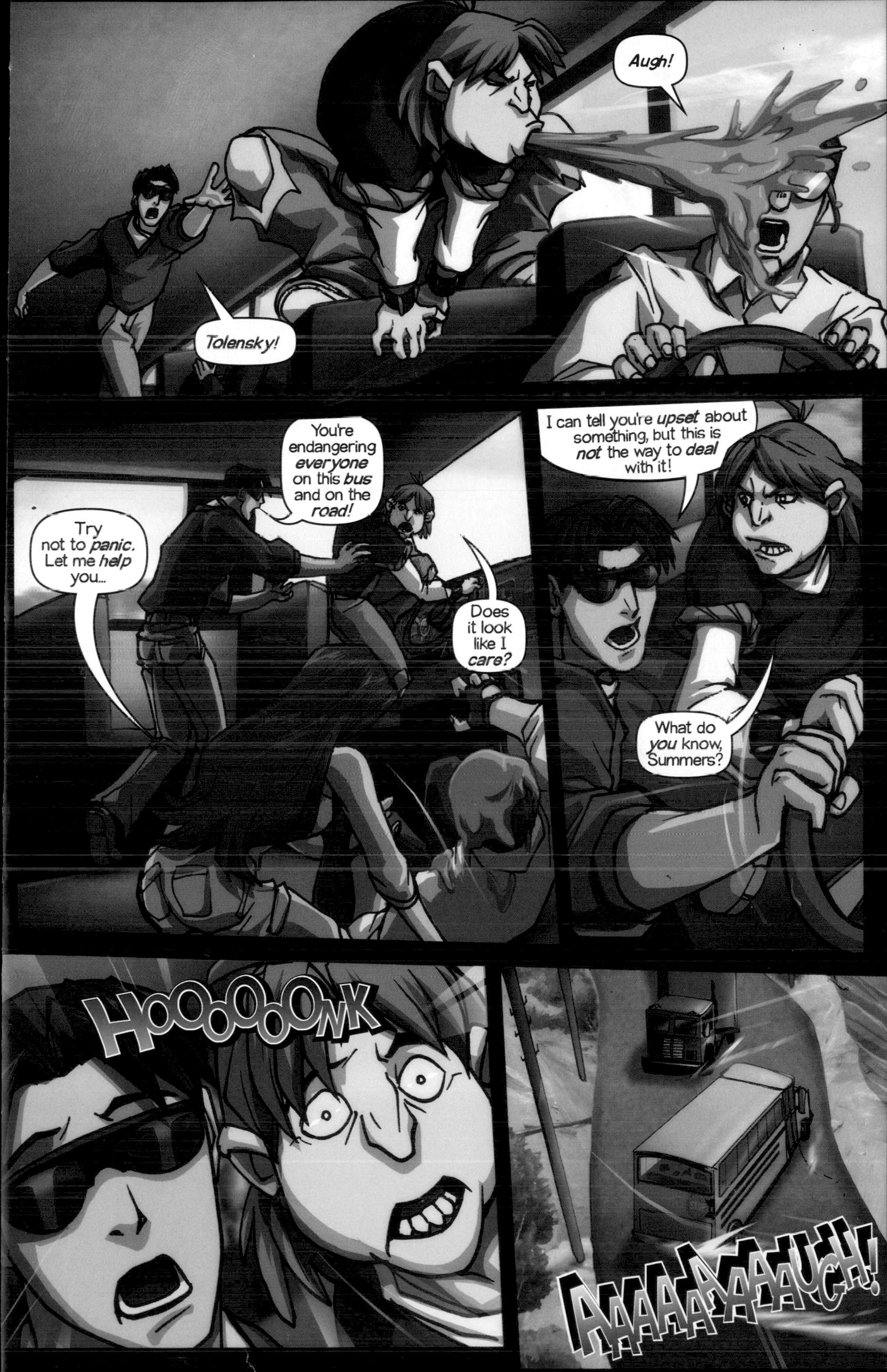

Augh!
Tolensky!
Try not to panic. Let me help you...
You're endangering everyone on this bus and on the road!
Does it look like I care?
I can tell you're upset about something, but this is not the way to deal with it!
What do you know, Summers?
HOOOOOONK
AAAAAAAAUGH!

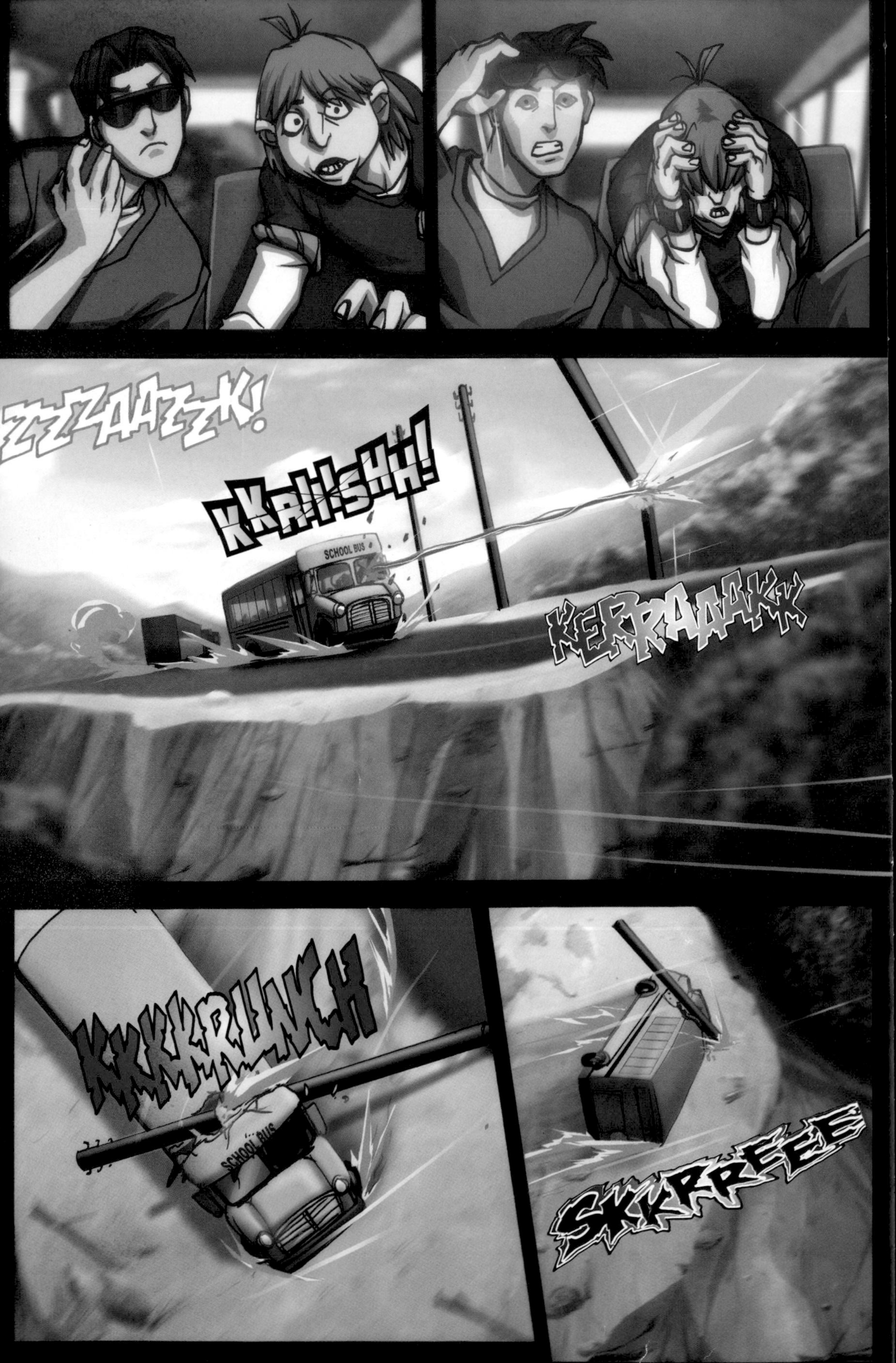
ZZZAAZZK!
KKRIISHH!
SCHOOL BUS
KERRAAAKK
KKKRUNCH
SCHOOL BUS
SKKRREEE

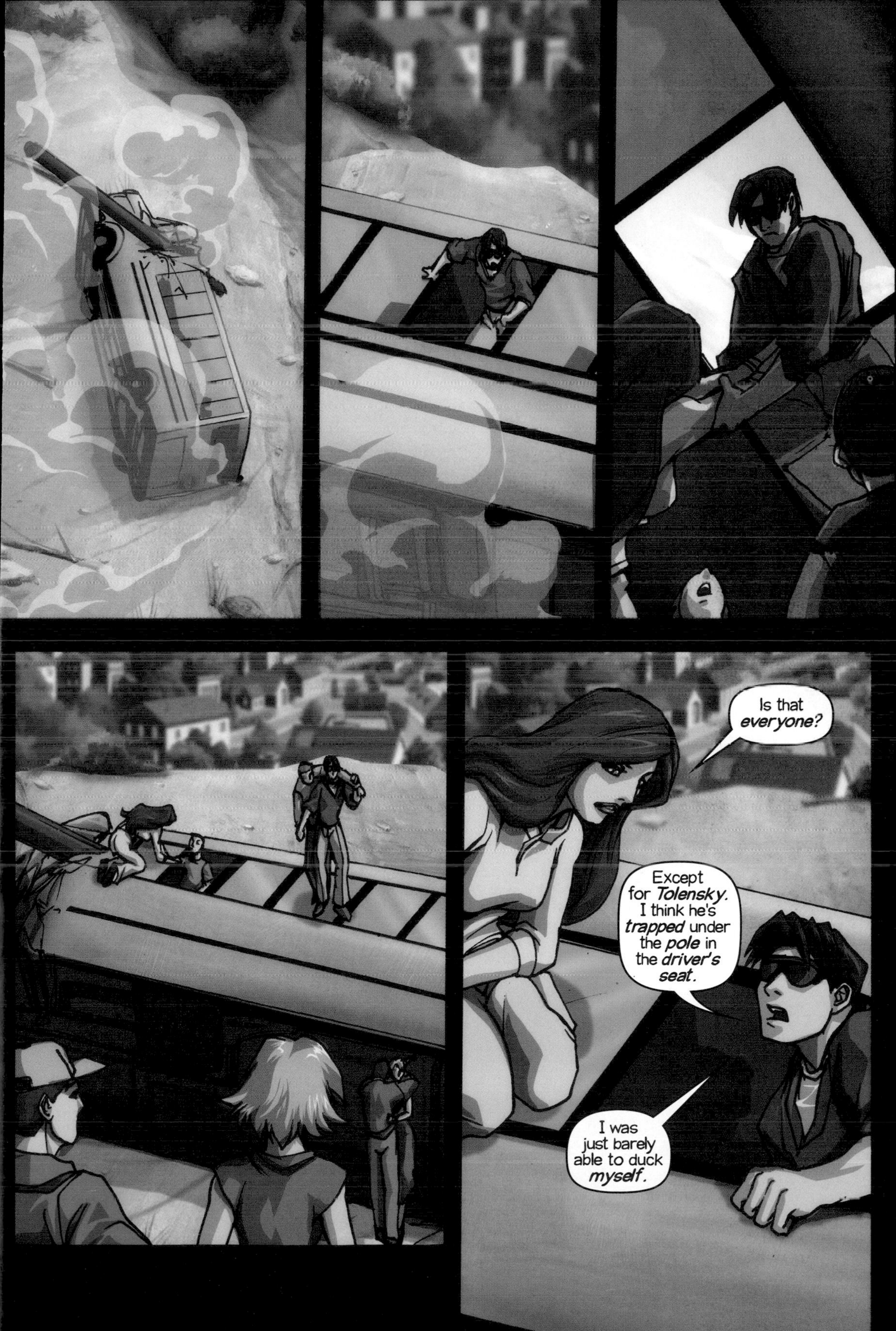
Is that *everyone?*
Except for *Tolensky.* I think he's *trapped* under the *pole* in the *driver's seat.*
I was just barely able to duck *myself.*

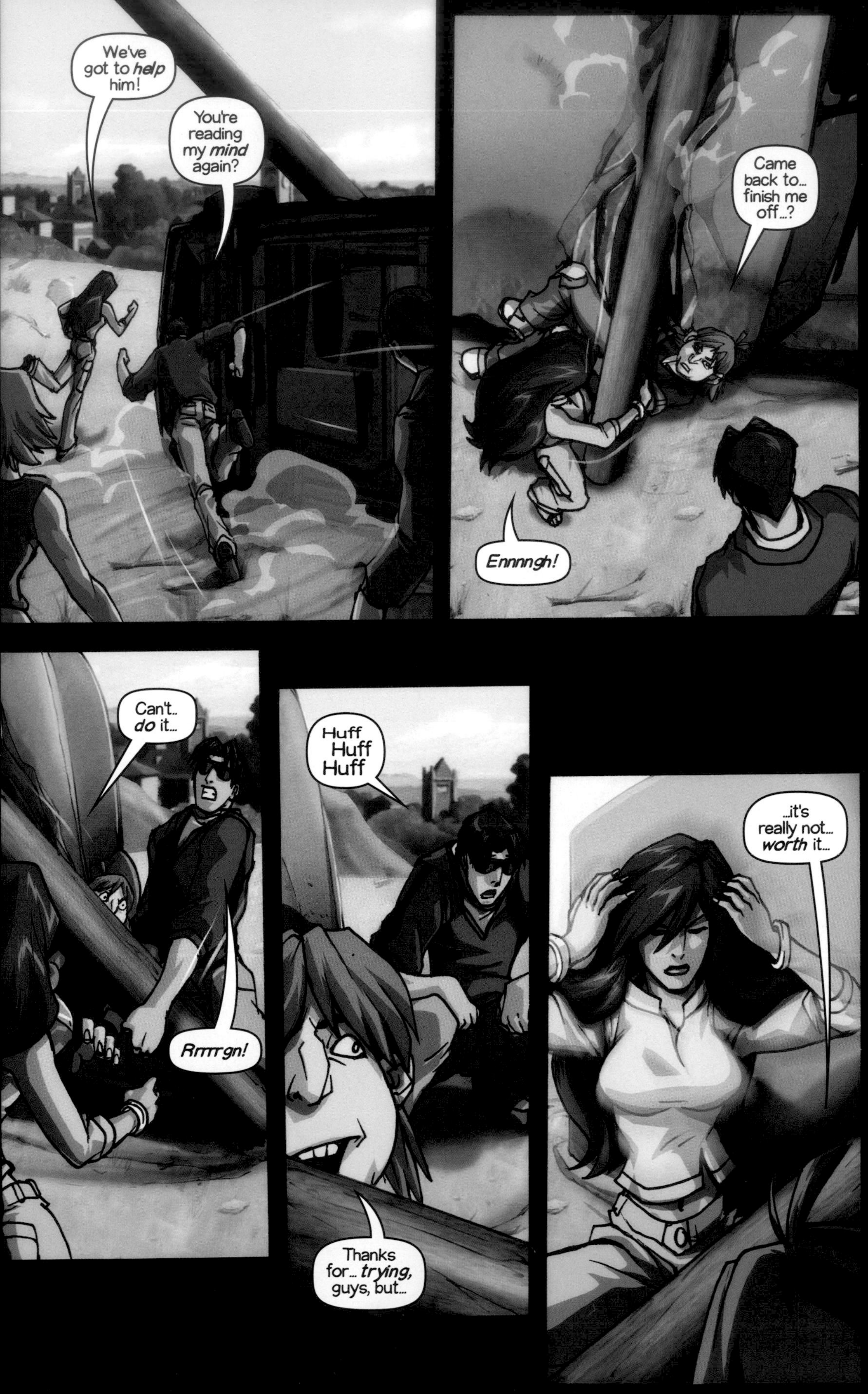
We've got to *help* him!
You're reading my *mind* again?
Came back to... finish me off...?
Ennnngh!
Can't.. *do* it...
Rrrrrgn!
Huff Huff Huff
Thanks for... *trying,* guys, but...
...it's really not... *worth* it...

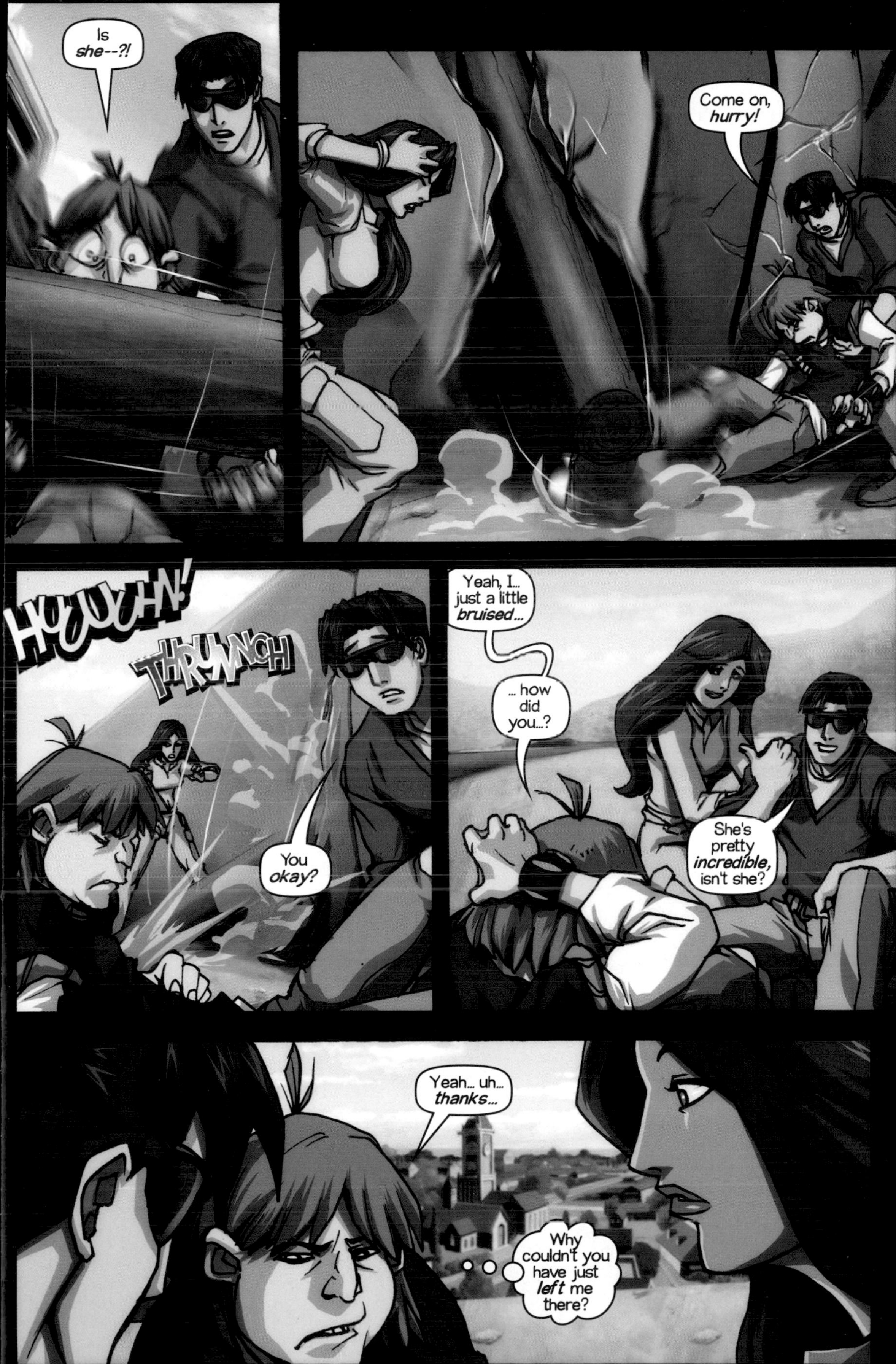
Is she--?!
Come on, hurry!
HUUUUHN!
THRUNNCH
You okay?
Yeah, I... just a little bruised...
... how did you...?
She's pretty incredible, isn't she?
Yeah... uh... thanks...
Why couldn't you have just left me there?

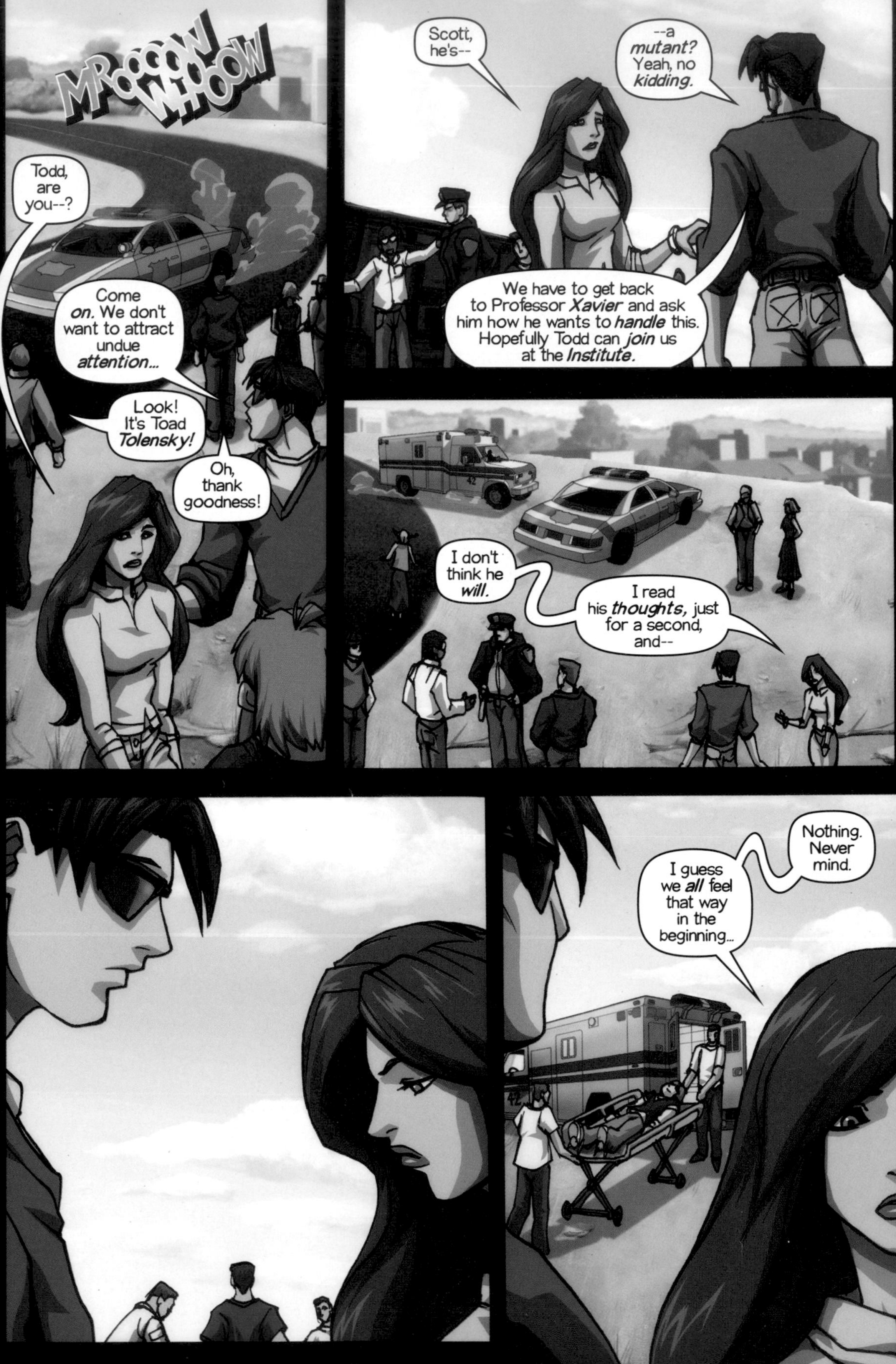
MROOOOW WHOOOW
Todd, are you--?
Come on. We don't want to attract undue attention...
Look! It's Toad Tolensky!
Oh, thank goodness!
Scott, he's--
--a mutant? Yeah, no kidding.
We have to get back to Professor Xavier and ask him how he wants to handle this. Hopefully Todd can join us at the Institute.
I don't think he will.
I read his thoughts, just for a second, and--
I guess we all feel that way in the beginning...
Nothing. Never mind.

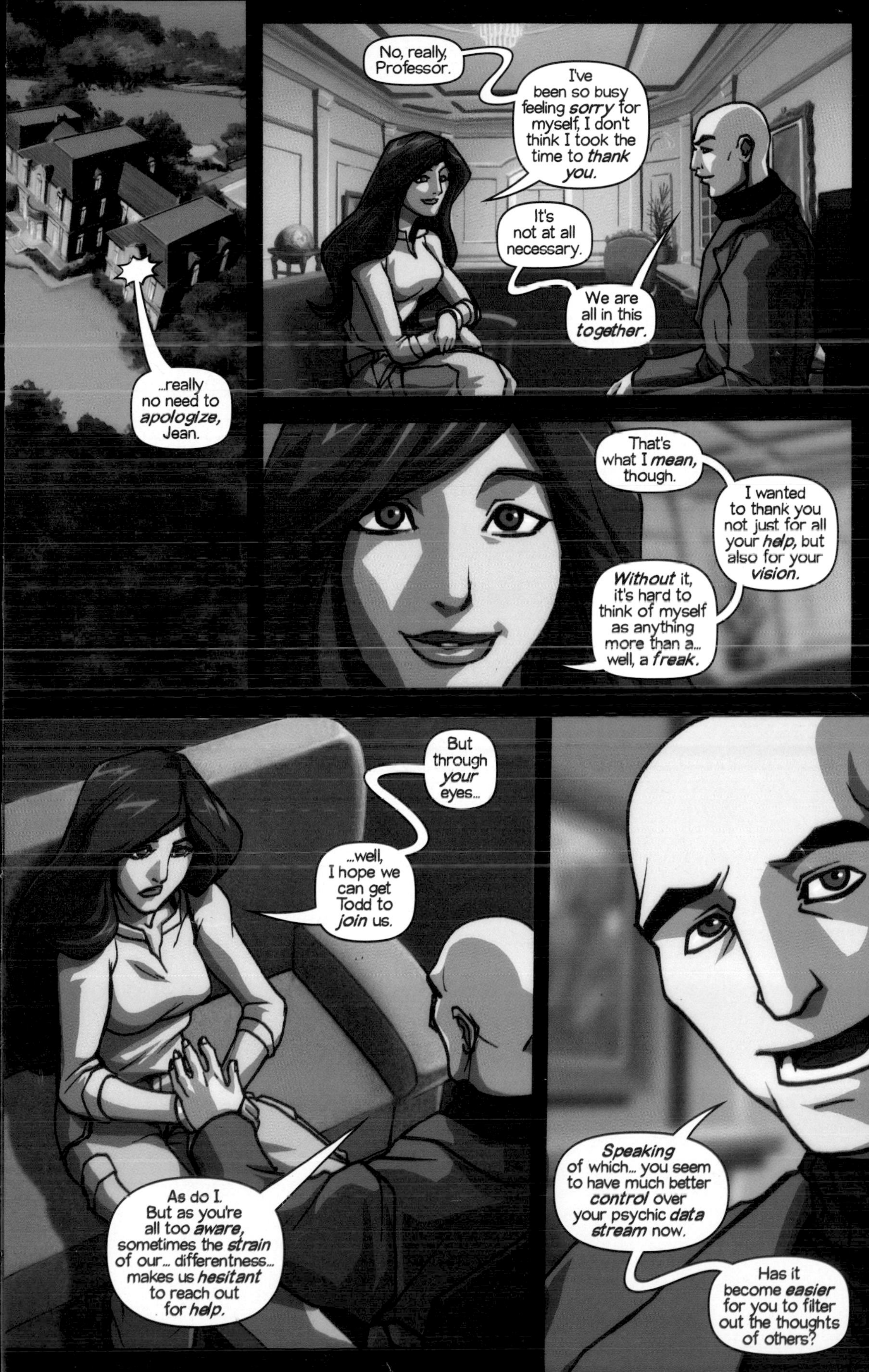
...really no need to *apologize,* Jean.
No, really, Professor.
I've been so busy feeling *sorry* for myself, I don't think I took the time to *thank you.*
It's not at all necessary.
We are all in this *together.*
That's what I *mean,* though.
I wanted to thank you not just for all your *help,* but also for your *vision.*
Without it, it's hard to think of myself as anything more than a... well, a *freak.*
But through *your* eyes...
...well, I hope we can get Todd to *join* us.
As do I. But as you're all too *aware,* sometimes the *strain* of our... differentness... makes us *hesitant* to reach out for *help.*
Speaking of which... you seem to have much better *control* over your psychic *data stream* now.
Has it become *easier* for you to filter out the thoughts of others?

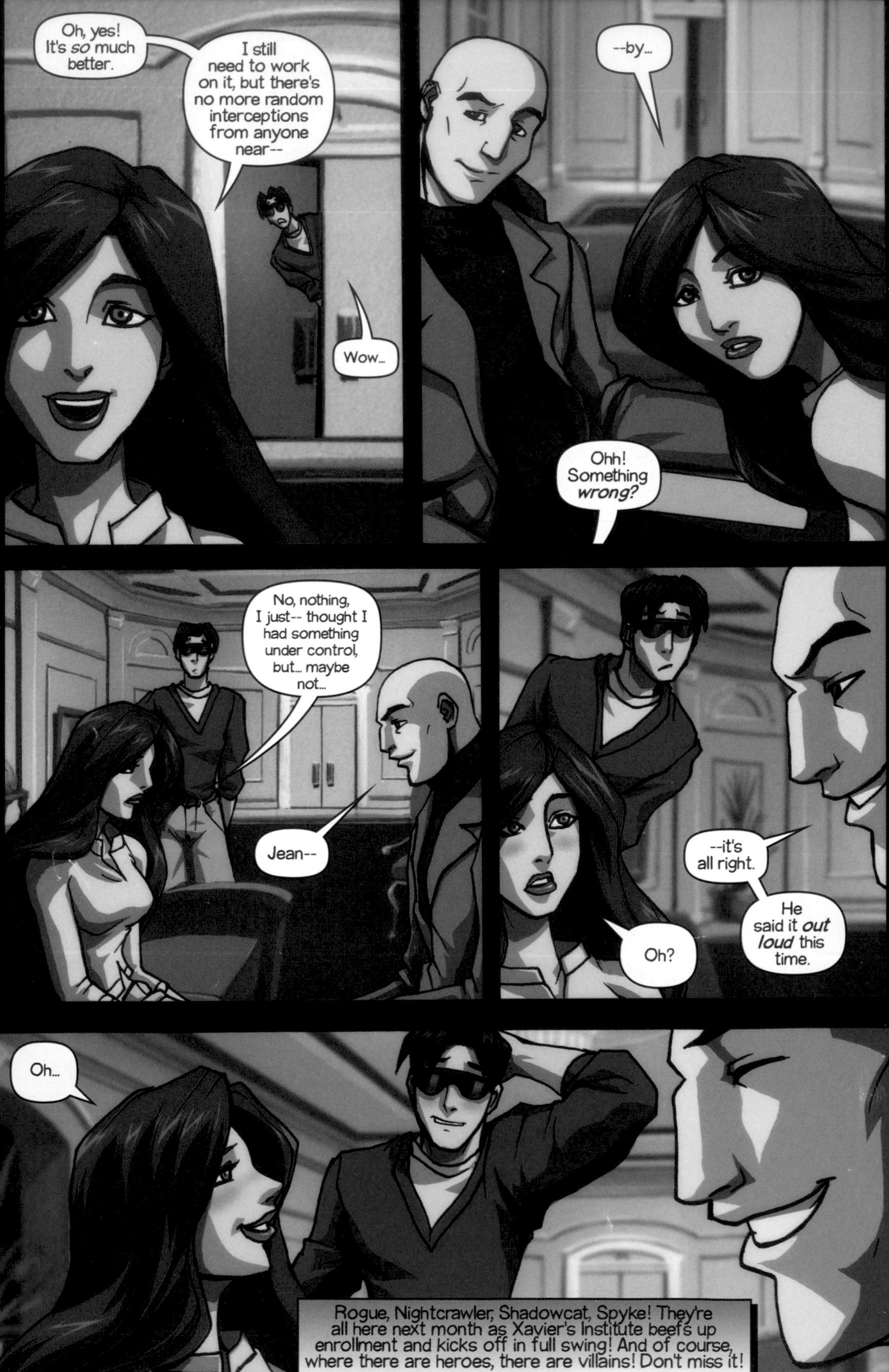

Oh, yes! It's *so* much better.
I still need to work on it, but there's no more random interceptions from anyone near--
Wow...
--by...
Ohh! Something ***wrong?***
No, nothing, I just-- thought I had something under control, but... maybe not...
Jean--
--it's all right.
Oh?
He said it ***out loud*** this time.
Oh...
Rogue, Nightcrawler, Shadowcat, Spyke! They're all here next month as Xavier's Institute beefs up enrollment and kicks off in full swing! And of course, where there are heroes, there are villains! Don't miss it!